THE SURF SCARE

By Michelle Nagler
Illustrated by Duendes del Sur

Hello Reader — Level 1

ISBN 0-439-44419-5

12 11 10 9   8/0

Designed by Maria Stasavage
Printed in the U.S.A.
First printing, May 2003

SCHOLASTIC INC.
New York Toronto London Auckland Sydney
Mexico City New Delhi Hong Kong Buenos Aires

"Does everyone have a ?"

asked 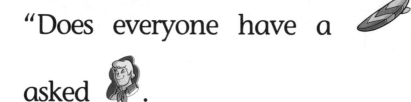.

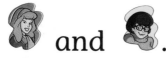 and his friends were entering

a surfing contest at the beach.

"We've got our 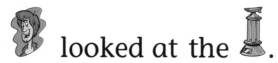 ," said

 and .

 looked at the .

"Wouldn't it be cool to win the

 ,  ?"

Steve the  blew his

🪈 . The surfing contest was

starting.

🧑‍🦱 went first. She stood up on

her 🏄 for a long time.

Next, 🧑 and 👩 did tricks on

their 🏄 🏄 .

Finally, it was 🧑 and 🐕 's

turn . . .

Big  came!

One  took the  sailing through the water.

The  moved very fast!  and  were scared.

Finally, the  hit a  and stopped.

 and  landed on the beach.

"That took us way out to sea," said . "This must be an ."

The beach was empty — except for some and . "Rare re rost?" asked .

"Yeah, we are lost," said . "Like, we have to find a way off this !"

thought he found a , but it was just a and two .

found a , some , and a small , but no way off the .

Then found a and . "Good idea, !" said . "I know what you're thinking."

"We can put a message in this 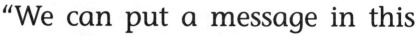," 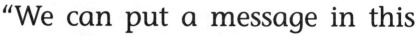 said, holding up a 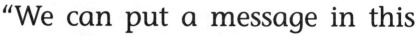 .

"Rave rus!" said 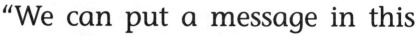 .

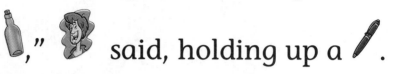 wrote SAVE US on the and put it in the .

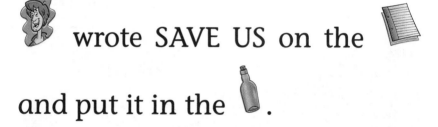 tossed the into the sea.

"Someone will find the  and rescue us!" said  .

had another idea.

"Maybe we can use the to get back to the beach!" he said.

 shook his head.

"Ro ray!" barked, pointing at the sea.

"Zoinks!" said . "Those are !"

Soon, and got hungry. sniffed the of food he had found.

"It's not , but it will do!" said .

They built a and cooked lunch. Suddenly, they heard a noise.

"Something is coming," said .

"!" said .

But it was , , and .

"Did you get our message in the ?" asked .

"No, we saw the smoke from your ," said .

"How did you get to our ?" asked . "With a ?"

"This is not an ," said .

"This is the other end of the beach — past the big ."

"Let's surf back!" said .

 shook his head. " !"

"Those are ," said . "They won't hurt us."

The gang got on the .

Another big came.

It took the back to the beach.

The blew his .

"Oh no," said . "What's wrong?"

Steve the held the 🏛. "You won the contest!"

"We were rescuing 🐕!" said 👩‍🦰.

"How did you fit on one 🏄?" asked Steve.

"Simple," said 👱. "We make a great team!"

"A great *surf* team!" said 👧.

🐕 barked. "Scooby-Dooby-Doo!"

Did you spot all the picture clues in this Scooby-Doo mystery?

Each picture clue is on a flash card. Ask a grown-up to cut out the flash cards. Then try reading the words on the back of the cards. The pictures will be your clue.

Reading is fun with Scooby-Doo!

Fred	surfboard
Daphne	Scooby
Shaggy	Velma

trophy	lifeguard
whistle	wave
rock	island

palm tree	shells
boat	can
crab	bottle

paper	pen
Scooby Snacks	fire
sharks	dolphins